To order additional copies of this book, contact:
Xlibris
1-888-795-4274
www.Xlibris.com
Orders@Xlibris.com

Happy

The Rubber Duck

BY RAY LACHANCE

"Evenings are my favorite time of the day," the little yellow rubber duck thought. "I can't wait to hear the sounds of the girls coming up the stairs for bath time. It gets lonely sitting on the tub with the other bath toys."

Mom and Dad would fill the tub with warm water, add the bubbles, and then put the toys in. Of course, he gets put in **first!** The two girls, Chloe and Jaedyn, love him. He makes them giggle and laugh. This is how he got his name "Happy."

He could hear the girls coming up the stairs with Mom. They were very excited to play in the tub. They always took turns playing with Happy.

Squeak squeak - Happy sounded out. Chloe would hold him up in the air, fly him around in the tub, and then – **Swoosh** - dive him into the water – **Splash!** Jaedyn just liked to watch Happy bob around in the bubbles and squeak him.

Bath time ended. The girls dried off, put on their PJ's, brushed their teeth, and off they went to their bedrooms. Dad came up to tuck them in, read stories, and give them a kiss. He then shut off the light and said, "Good night. I love you my little ducklings!"

In the meantime, Mom was busy cleaning up. She placed all of the toys on the side of the tub. However, this time, she put Happy up on the windowsill to dry. All was quiet. There Happy was, just sitting on the sill looking out the window. He was glad Mom put him up there.

There were many amazing things out there to see! The sun was beginning to set. There was a big Maple tree outside the window with a long branch. A large black crow flew down and landed on it. *Caw, caw, caw,* it cried out. Happy thought the crow was calling to his friends flying up in the sky.

Down below, two people were jogging with their dog, who was on a leash. Happy could see birds pecking in the grass. "I guess they are eating insects?" he said. "I wish I could fly so I could see even more!"

Soon it became dark. A bright moon shone in the night behind some clouds. A bat flew by. The house became very, very quiet. The only sounds heard were from Mom and Dad retiring for the evening.

The night seemed long and lonely. "I am not snuggled up to the other toys on the tub. I miss them," Happy thought. To his relief, morning soon came. A ray of sun came through the window and cast a shadow across the floor. "I can see myself on the floor!"

Before long, Mom and Dad woke up and went downstairs. Chloe and Jaedyn came into the bathroom to get ready for school. The girls washed up and were brushing their teeth when Chloe looked up at Happy on the sill. She giggled and said, "Good morning Happy. How did you get up there?"

Jaedyn, in the meantime, went to the window, scooped Happy up, and gave him a great big squeeze. **_Squeak squeak –_** sounded his little yellow body. "Now you be a good little rubber duck today Happy," said Jaedyn. She put him back up on the windowsill in front of the open window. All was quiet again.

As Happy sat there, many birds flew by the window. Some landed in the tree and still others landed on the ground. "I wish I could fly," he thought

Suddenly, that big old black crow swooped down and landed on the branch just outside the window. Happy could see his shiny eyes, a powerful looking beak, pretty black feathers, and wings.

"Hello," said Crow, "what are you doing up here?" Crow was scary looking at first, but he seemed friendly enough. "I am just looking out the window," Happy explained. "Is this where you live?" asked Crow.

"Yes," Happy said, "Mom put me up here last night. It has been fun watching birds, dragonflies, bumble bees, butterflies, and geese fly by."

"What does it feel like to fly Mr. Crow?" Happy asked, "I wish I could fly like you and the other birds!" Crow replied, "I see that you do not have wings. Hmmm...I have just the idea that will let you see many things from the sky." "That will be so much fun." Happy said. Crow sped off shouting, "I will be right back."

Crow knew exactly where to go and what to find. Nearby there was a playground with a sandbox full of toys. He had spotted it before while flying and searching for food. In the sandbox there was a soldier with a parachute folded up on his back. "This will work just fine," said Crow to himself.

So Crow pulled the parachute off the soldier with his beak. He examined it very carefully for any tears, rips, or holes. Satisfied, he gripped it tight and **Swish** – off he flew back to the window where Happy was waiting patiently.

"I am back," said Crow. "What is that in your beak?" Happy asked. "It is called a parachute. This will allow you to see the wonderful world from way up high. I will strap it onto your back. Then I will fly you up in the air, count to three, and then pull a cord," explained Crow.

Crow continued, "You will slowly float to the ground. This will feel just like flying." "Wow! This is going to be exciting. Is it safe?" asked Happy. "Are you ready?" asked Crow. "I think so," stuttered the nervous duck.

Crow put the handle of the parachute in his beak and lifted Happy off the ledge. In an instant, they were flying up past houses and trees. They headed up, up, up high into the sky. Happy could see many things below him. Crow flew still higher and higher.

Finally Crow leveled off and circled in the air. "Are you ready Happy?" asked Crow. "I...I think so," Happy gulped. "On the count of three, I will pull the rip cord, the chute will open, and you will begin to fall to the ground," explained Crow. And just like that, Crow pulled the rip cord and down went Happy toward the ground...then...***Poof*** - the chute opened up.

"Oh no!" Happy kept saying as he began floating downward. "This is fun, but really, really, scary." The breeze kept moving him to the right, then to the left, up, and then down which made his ride really terrifying!

All was quiet in the sky. Happy could see houses, barns, animals, and a large playground in the distance. Down, down, down, Happy floated. "I can see birds flying just like me!" Happy shouted nervously.

Finally the parachute came to a soft landing on the grass. "I landed, I landed!" Happy shouted. **Swish –** down flew Crow. "Congratulations Happy," he said. Crow explained that he now needed to take the parachute off and return it back to the sandbox. "Did you like flying?" Crow asked. Happy said he did, since he did not want to hurt his new friend's feelings. "I am sorry that I cannot return you back to the sill," said Crow.

"That's okay. Thank you anyways Mr. Crow. You are a true friend. I hope to see you again sometime!" Happy exclaimed. "Goodbye my friend!" said Crow. **Swish** - off went Crow to new adventures. Happy just sat there in the grass. All was quiet once more.

Suddenly, Happy heard the school bus. Lights were flashing, the door opened up, and out came Chloe and Jaedyn. The bus sped off. The girls came up the walkway talking, giggling, and laughing. They both stopped in their tracks. "Happy! What on earth are you doing down here in the grass?" asked Chloe.

"I bet the wind blew Happy out the window," Jaedyn said. "I think you are correct," said Chloe. Jaedyn picked Happy up and squeezed him - *Squeak squeak*. "He is alright!" they both agreed. "Let's bring him upstairs to the side of the tub where he belongs," said Chloe..

So the girls went upstairs and placed Happy back on the side of the tub with all of his other toy friends. "I am so glad to be back," he thought. Happy looked up at the windowsill remembering all that he had seen.

"Wishes are nice, but I am very glad to be home. I may not be able to fly, swallow, or talk, but I can go **- *Squeak squeak* –** while I play in the water with Chloe, Jaedyn, and my toy friends," thought Happy. That little yellow rubber duck just snuggled up to the other toys very, very, content. And all was quiet again.

The end

Printed in the United States
By Bookmasters